Bedtime Stories

Cover illustrated by Sara Gianassi
Illustrated by Sara Gianassi, Xuan Le, Hannah Tolson, Hannah Peck,
Tiziana Longo, Victoria Assanelli, Julianna Swaney, Katie Wilson,
Claire McElfatrick, Luisa Uribe, Livia Coloji, Alette Straathof,
Abigail Dela Cruz, John Joven, and Morgan Huff.

Selected stories retold by Anne Rooney, Mandy Archer,
Catherine Allison, Lilly Holland, Etta Saunders, Karen Ball, Claire Sipi,
and Jane Riordan.

Every effort has been made to
acknowledge the contributors of this book.
If we have made any errors, we will be pleased
to rectify them in future editions.

Created 2018 by Parragon Books, Ltd.

ISBN 978-1-64638-023-7

Bedtime Stories

A Timeless Collection of
Stories and Rhymes
to Share

PaRRagon.

Contents
Stories and Fables

Songs and Rhymes

Stories and Fables

Little Red Riding Hood

There was once a sweet and happy little girl whose granny had made her a lovely red cape with a hood. The little girl loved it so much that she wore it everywhere she went. Soon everyone became so used to her wearing it that they called her "Little Red Riding Hood."

"Little Red Riding Hood," said her mother one morning, "Granny is not feeling very well. Take her this basket of food and see if you can cheer her up."

Little Red Riding Hood loved to visit her granny, so she took the basket of food and set off right away.

"Go straight to Granny's house and don't talk to any strangers!" her mother called after her.

"I won't, don't worry," sang Little Red Riding Hood as she went merrily on her way.

Little Red Riding Hood skipped off through the woods with the basket swinging on her arm. The sun was shining, the birds were chirping in the treetops, and she didn't have a care in the world. After a while, she spotted a wolf peering at her through the trees.

"Well, hello there," said the wolf in a silky voice. "And where are you off to on this fine morning?"

"I'm going to visit my granny," replied Little Red Riding Hood, forgetting her mother's warning. "She's not feeling well and I'm taking her this food to make her better."

The wolf licked his lips. "And where might your dear old granny live?" he asked.

"She lives in a cottage at the other side of the woods," replied Little Red Riding Hood. "This path leads right to her door."

"Is that so?" said the wolf. "How very interesting."

There were some beautiful wild flowers growing in the woods and Little Red Riding Hood stopped to admire them.

"Why don't you pick a pretty posy for your granny?" suggested the wolf.

"What a lovely idea," said Little Red Riding Hood, and she stooped down to pick some. She was too busy choosing the prettiest flowers to notice the wolf slinking off down the path.

The wolf's tummy rumbled as he trotted through the woods. When at last he reached the end of the path, he saw a little cottage just as Little Red Riding Hood had described. The wicked old wolf knocked on the door.

"Come on in, my darling," called the grandmother, thinking that it was Little Red Riding Hood.

The wolf walked into the cottage. Before the grandmother had a chance to call for help the wicked creature opened his huge jaws and swallowed her whole! Then he climbed into her bed, pulled the covers up under his chin, and waited.

Soon, Little Red Riding Hood reached her granny's house with her basket of food and a bunch of wild flowers. "Won't Granny be pleased to see me!" she thought, as she knocked on the door.

"Come right in, my darling," replied a strange, croaky voice.

"Poor Granny," thought Little Red Riding Hood. "She doesn't sound at all well!"

Little Red Riding Hood looked in the kitchen, but her granny wasn't there. She looked in the living room, but Granny wasn't there either. Finally she went into her granny's bedroom, and she gasped in surprise.

"Why, Granny," exclaimed Little Red Riding Hood. "Your ears are absolutely enormous!"

"All the better to hear you with, my dear," replied a low, silky voice.

"But, Granny," gulped Little Red Riding Hood. "Your eyes, they're as big as saucers!"

"All the better to see you with, my dear," replied a rumbling, growly voice.

Little Red Riding Hood took a step toward the bed.

"And your teeth are so … pointed!" gasped Little Red Riding Hood.

"All the better to EAT you with!" snarled a loud, hungry voice.

The wolf leaped out of bed and gobbled up Little Red Riding Hood in one big **GULP!**

13

A woodcutter chopping nearby heard some suspicious growling noises coming from inside the little cottage.

"I don't like the sound of that!" he thought. He took his ax and creeped into the grandmother's house to investigate. He tiptoed into the bedroom and found the wolf fast asleep… with his tummy ready to explode.

"You wicked old wolf," said the woodcutter. "I'll teach you a lesson!"

He tipped the stunned wolf upside down and shook him as hard as he could. To his surprise, out fell a very dazed Little Red Riding Hood, followed by her poor old granny.

"Thank you for saving us!" said Little Red Riding Hood. "Are you OK, Granny?"

But Granny was looking at the wolf furiously. "I'll give you a piece of my mind," she said.

She chased the wolf out of her bedroom, through the cottage, and out into the woods, with the woodcutter and Little Red Riding Hood following close behind her.

The wolf never returned, and Little Red Riding Hood never spoke to strangers ever again.

The King's Secret

Once upon a time, there was a king with an embarrassing secret. In place of his own ears, he had a pair of huge, hairy donkey ears! The king was very proud and didn't want people to laugh at him, so he used his hair and crown to hide them.

He kept the secret for years, but one day his trusted barber retired, and he had no choice but to invite someone new to the palace to cut his hair …

Barber Babek was honored when he was called on and was determined to make a good impression. It was very quiet in the throne room, so Babek decided to tell the king a joke. All his customers loved his jokes.

As he cut off a lock of hair, he cleared his throat. "What do you call a donkey with three legs?" he asked. When the king didn't reply, he supplied the punch line: "A wonky!"

"Just finish cutting my hair," the king said sharply.

The barber swallowed, and continued to trim the king's hair through his gold crown. It would have been much easier without it, but the king had refused to take it off.

Babek adjusted the crown ever so slightly, and as he did so … **POP!** Up shot a long, brown, hairy ear.

"You have donkey ears!" Babek cried, his scissors clattering to the marble floor.

"You must keep this secret to yourself," the king said. "Or else. Now leave!"

For weeks afterwards, Babek struggled to cut people's hair. All the customers wanted to hear his jokes, but Babek didn't trust himself to speak at all. People stopped coming to him to have their hair cut. Babek was going to be ruined! He had to get this secret out somehow.

One night when he could bear it no longer, he ran to a field and slumped down beside a tree. He just needed to say the secret out loud, so he whispered it into a hole in the bark. He didn't notice the breeze that made the cornstalks shiver.

"The king has..." The rest of his words disappeared into the tree trunk and Babek sighed with relief.

Babek went back to his shop and started telling his jokes again. But soon a whisper began to move around the city streets.

"The king has donkey ears..." it said. Babek heard the words and recognized his own voice, carried on the wind.

Soon the townsfolk began repeating the words to each other, and their voices became louder and louder.

Babek tried to run away from them, but the words followed him down the street and flew into the windows of the royal palace where the king was dozing.

The king was woken by the whispers and stormed
out onto the stone balcony. "Babek!" he roared. "You didn't
keep my secret!"

"I tried to," the barber called up. "But the wind got
the better of me."

The Flying Trunk

Once there was a merchant so rich he could have paved a street in silver, but instead he chose to leave all his money to his idle son.

After enjoying the high life, the son soon found that all his father's money had vanished. The people who had claimed to be his friends disappeared, too, and the son was left with nothing but an old trunk with a mysterious note saying, "Pack up and be off!"

The merchant's son was amazed to discover that the old trunk could fly! He climbed in, closed the lid, and flew high into the sky, leaving his troubles behind.

At last the trunk descended and he found himself in a foreign land. Standing on a hill on the horizon was a magnificent palace.

"Who lives in that palace?" he asked a passing stranger.

"The king's daughter," came the reply. "It has been prophesied that a man will make her desperately unhappy so no one is allowed to visit, except the king and queen."

Hearing this, the merchant's son had an idea. That evening he flew up to the palace roof and into the princess's room. He was immediately struck by her beauty.

"Do not be afraid," he told her gently. "I am a wise magician descended from the sky."

The lonely princess was excited to meet someone other than her parents. She was entranced by the stranger's tales of mermaids in dark-blue seas and princesses on magical snow-clad mountains. She believed this magician had been sent just for her and readily agreed to his proposal of marriage.

"You must come to meet my parents at once," she told him. "I'm sure the king and queen will be pleased to hear I am to marry a magician." And then she gave him some advice. "They are very fond of stories. My mother likes them to be moral and my father likes them to be merry."

"I shall bring a tale as my bridal present," he replied confidently. And before he flew away, the princess gave him a gift of a sword studded in gold.

"I shall exchange this for more fine clothes," he thought as he waved his princess farewell.

When the merchant's son arrived at the palace a few days later, the princess proudly introduced him to the king and queen as a magician and storyteller.

"There was once a bundle of matches," he began. "They lay on a mantelpiece between a tinderbox and an iron saucepan. They often talked about their youth."

The king and queen smiled in approval.

"The matches were proud that they had once been branches on a towering fir tree," the merchant's son continued. "They boasted how the trunk of the tree became a mainmast of a magnificent ship that sailed around the world. And they told how the birds would relate stories of far-off lands they had visited. The matches felt they were far too respectable and impressive to live in a kitchen."

"But where is the merriment?" asked the king.

"Soon," replied the merchant's son, continuing. "The iron saucepan and the tinderbox shared the stories of their own youthful days, and others in the kitchen began to join in.

"Each of the inhabitants of the kitchen felt that *they* were from the most respectable background, and one after the other they boasted and demonstrated their usefulness.

"Before anyone else could tell their tale, the maid came in to light the fire. The whole kitchen watched in silence as she struck the matches. How they blazed up!

"'Now,' thought the matches, 'everyone can see *we* are the most superior by the dazzling light we bring.'

"But no sooner had they thought this, their light vanished as the maid completed her task. The matches were burnt out!"

The king and queen laughed out loud and applauded loudly.

"You shall marry our daughter on Monday," the king declared.

The night before the wedding the whole city was illuminated and cakes and buns were thrown to the people in the street.

"I should play my part," thought the merchant's son, so he bought some fireworks and set them off one by one as he flew into the air in his trunk.

The crowd jumped and roared with delight as rockets and fountains of light filled the sky in honor of their princess marrying a magician.

Later, the merchant's son hid the trunk in the woods and set off into the city to hear what the people were saying about him.

"I hear the magician has eyes like sparkling stars," one in the crowd told him.

"And a beard like foaming water!" said another.

Happy with his evening's work, and excited about his marriage the next day, the merchant's son returned to the woods.

But disaster faced him. A spark from a firework had ignited the trunk and it now lay in ashes. The merchant's son could never fly again, and so could no longer pretend to be the magician he had promised his bride.

Every day the princess sat on the palace roof waiting for her magician. He never appeared, and the prophecy came true.

Aladdin

Once upon a time, a boy called Aladdin lived with his mother. They were so poor that every day it was a struggle to find enough money for food.

One day a man came to their shack saying he was Aladdin's long-lost uncle. When he said he would help Aladdin make his fortune, Aladdin and his mother were delighted.

Aladdin traveled with him into the desert until they came to a rock. The man pushed it aside, revealing a hidden cave.

"You must climb down into this cave and fetch a lamp that you will find there," he said. "Bring it to me. Don't touch anything except the lamp."

Aladdin was afraid, but he didn't dare argue with his uncle. He took a deep breath and climbed into the cave.

As soon as he was through the entrance his eyes grew wide with wonder.

All around, piles of gold and jewels stretched from floor to ceiling. Gemstones glittered in the dim light. Just one ruby would make Aladdin and his mother rich. But he did as he had promised and touched nothing. At last he found a dull, brass lamp.

"Surely this can't be it." Aladdin thought, but he took it back to his uncle.

When he got to the opening, he found he couldn't climb out of the cave holding the lamp.

"Pass it to me," his uncle said, "then I will help you out."

"Help me out first, Uncle," Aladdin replied, "and then I will give you the lamp."

"No!" the man shouted. "First give me the lamp!"

When Aladdin refused, he became angry. He rolled the stone over the cave opening, trapping Aladdin.

"Uncle!" Aladdin shouted, "Let me out!"

"Hah!" the man shouted. "I'm not your uncle, fool. I'm a sorcerer! You can stay in there and die if you won't give me the lamp!"

Aladdin wrung his hands in despair. As he did so, he accidentally rubbed the lamp he was holding. Suddenly, a genie sprang out.

"I am the genie of the lamp. What do you require, O master?" The genie bowed. Aladdin was astonished, but he thought quickly.

"Please take me home to my mother," he said. And immediately he was outside his mother's house. He told her everything that had happened, and she hugged him with relief.

"Oh, but Aladdin," she cried, "we are still poor!"

The next day, Aladdin looked at the lamp he had fetched from the cave. "It doesn't look like much," he thought, and he started to polish it, hoping the genie would appear once more. As soon as he rubbed the lamp, the genie appeared.

"I am the genie of the lamp. What do you require, O master?" the genie asked. This time, Aladdin knew what to do.

He asked the genie to bring food and money so that he and his mother could live in comfort.

Life went on happily, and Aladdin had no need to summon the genie. Then one day, Aladdin saw the beautiful daughter of the emperor. He fell in love and felt that he couldn't live without her. But how could he marry a princess?

Aladdin thought and thought, and finally he had an idea. He rubbed the lamp, and when the genie appeared he asked him to send beautiful gifts to the princess. He needed to meet her!

When the princess called Aladdin to the palace to thank him for the gifts, she fell in love with him. They were married, and Aladdin asked the genie to build them a beautiful home.

Hearing that a wealthy stranger had married the princess, the sorcerer guessed that Aladdin must have escaped from the cave with the lamp.

One day, when Aladdin was out, the sorcerer disguised himself as a poor tradesman. He stood in the marketplace calling out, "New lamps for old! New lamps for old!"

Aladdin's wife remembered the ugly brass lamp that Aladdin kept and took it to the man.

The sorcerer snatched it from her, rubbed the lamp and commanded the genie to make her fall out of love with Aladdin.

The genie hadn't even replied before the princess's expression changed. "I hate Aladdin! What was I thinking?" she said.

"Good," cackled the sorcerer. "You can be my wife from now on. And when the boy comes home, we'll get the genie to drop him in the sea."

When Aladdin returned, he was shocked to find his wife hand in hand with the sorcerer. "My love, get away from him!" Aladdin exclaimed.

"She's mine now, boy," said the sorcerer, rubbing the lamp until the genie appeared.

"What do you require, O master?" asked the genie.

"Genie, dump this boy in the ocean. Make sure he drowns."

But the genie was looking at Aladdin! "I only serve one master," he said. The princess had been pretending all along!

"Genie," said Aladdin quickly, "shut this sorcerer in the cave for a thousand years— that will teach him a lesson!"

With the sorcerer gone, Aladdin and the princess were safe again. They lived long and happy lives together and never needed to call on the genie again.

The Magic Porridge Pot

A long time ago there was a little girl called Abigail, who lived with her mother in a rickety house in a quiet village. The family was very poor, and some days there was no more than a crumb to eat. Although her life was hard, Abigail was good and kind and everyone loved her.

One hungry day, Abigail's mother sent her into the forest to look for blackberries. Abigail searched all day, yet didn't find a single berry for her basket. She was on her way home when she met a mysterious old woman.

"Take this," said the woman, kindly, handing her a bright copper pot. "If you're ever hungry say 'Boil, little pot' and it will feed you well. Then say 'Stop, little pot' and it will do as you ask."

Before Abigail could thank the woman or ask who she was, she disappeared in a swirl of leaves.

Abigail ran as fast as she could all the way home to her hungry mother.

"Boil, little pot," she said and, sure enough, the pot began to rattle and bubble. A delicious smell filled the room and soon there was hot, sweet porridge for their supper.

Abigail's mother laughed in delight, and they ate and ate until they could eat no more.

"Stop, little pot," commanded Abigail, and they watched as the pot fell still and quiet on the table once more.

The same thing happened every day that week. For the first time Abigail and her mother didn't have to worry about food — Abigail told the little pot to boil whenever they were hungry. They grew healthy and strong with plump, rosy cheeks.

One day, when Abigail was out fetching wood, her mother decided to get the evening meal ready.

"Boil, little pot," she said, and the pot filled with porridge. But she couldn't remember the magic words to stop the pot, and it became so full that it started to spill over!

"Enough, little pot!" she cried, but that didn't work. "Please cease, little pot!" she said, but that didn't work either.

Soon the floor was covered in sticky porridge, and Abigail's mother ran out of the house. It wasn't long before the porridge was as high as the windows... then the roof... and finally it came pouring out of the chimney and began to fill the street.

Abigail's mother watched in despair as one by one, all the houses in the village filled up with porridge.

As the sun set, Abigail returned from the forest. What a sight awaited her—her dear village was covered in porridge!

Abigail guessed what had happened right away. "Stop, little pot!" she called, and at last it did.

The villagers had run far away from their homes to avoid the flood, and now gazed at the river of porridge keeping them from their beds. There was only one thing to do…it was time for a feast!

Beauty and the Beast

There was once a rich merchant who had three daughters. The youngest daughter had a kind heart, unlike her jealous sisters. She was called Beauty.

One winter, the merchant's ships vanished in a storm. He lost all his money and was forced to move into a tiny little cottage. The two elder daughters wept in anger, fearing no one would wish to marry them any longer. They would stay in bed all day, while Beauty rose at four each morning and cleaned the house and cooked their meals.

Then one day, the merchant received good news. One of his ships had been found, which meant he would have money again. He immediately set off for town.

"Bring me back a velvet cape," demanded the eldest sister.

"And I'll have a silk gown," added the second sister.

"What about you, Beauty?" asked her father kindly.

"Please bring me a rose, Father," said Beauty politely as she kissed her father goodbye. She worried terribly about him and longed for his safe return.

When the merchant arrived in town, he discovered that it was not his ship that had been found after all. With a heavy heart he rode back, failing to notice the snow had begun to fall thickly. Soon he was lost. He wandered for hours, and when night fell, he began to despair. At last, he spotted a golden light coming from a great castle.

Pushing on the open door, he soon found himself inside a dining hall where a fire blazed and a table was laid for one person.

But there was no one to greet him. At last he said to himself, "I can wait no longer. Surely the kind master will pardon me if I eat my meal alone."

After a good night's sleep, the merchant set off. He made his way through a scented rose garden and was reminded of Beauty's request. As he broke off a single red rose, there was a thunderous roar, and a hideous creature appeared before him.

"So this is how you repay my kindness!" the creature snarled. "I saved your life, and in thanks you choose to steal from me. You deserve to die."

"Forgive me, Lord," begged the merchant. "I only wanted to pluck a rose for my youngest daughter."

"Call me Beast," snapped the creature. "I will spare your life if one of your daughters comes to stay with me of her own free will. But if none of them agrees, you must return within three months."

With a sad heart, the merchant agreed.

After hearing her father's story, Beauty persuaded him to take her to the Beast's castle.

When she arrived, she could hardly dare look at the creature. But Beauty soon came to realize that he had a good heart.

One evening as he joined her for dinner, the Beast asked her, "Do you find me ugly?"

And for the first time Beauty looked at his face.

"Yes, but you are very kind," she replied honestly.

The Beast seemed pleased by her answer and suddenly asked if she would be his wife.

"No, Beast," she replied simply. And the Beast let out a painful cry.

As the time passed, Beauty came to enjoy her life at the castle. She had everything she needed. As a sign of his love for her, the Beast gave Beauty a magic mirror to show her what was happening at home.

One day as she looked into the mirror, she saw that her father was ill.

"I must go to my father," she told the Beast. "If you let me leave, I promise I will return."

Heartened by these words, the Beast agreed. "Take your mirror with you," he said. "And remember, if you do not return in one week, I shall die of grief."

Beauty's father was overjoyed to see her, and he soon became well again. The foolish sisters had both married but were unhappy, so they tricked Beauty into staying longer than the week.

One day when Beauty was looking in her magic mirror, she saw the Beast was ill. She knew she had to return. Arriving back at the castle, she found him close to death.

"You broke your promise," the Beast whispered, "and now I must die."

"No! No!" cried Beauty in anguish. And at that moment she knew she loved him. "I want to be your wife," she pleaded.

And as her tears fell onto the Beast's face, a bright light dazzled her. Suddenly, standing before her was the most handsome man she had ever set eyes on.

"Where is the Beast?" she cried.

"I was your Beast," smiled the young man. "But by choosing to stay with me and promising to be my wife, you have broken the spell that has cursed me."

Beauty and her prince were soon married. Beauty moved back into the castle, where they lived happily ever after.

The Elves and the Shoemaker

There was once an old shoemaker who lived with his wife. Although they worked from dawn until dusk every day, they were very poor.

"We have only enough leather to make one more pair of shoes to sell," the shoemaker told his wife one evening.

"What will become of us then?" asked the shoemaker's wife. "How can we live without money?"

The shoemaker shook his head sadly. He cut out the leather and left it on his workbench, ready to start work the next morning. Then the couple went to bed with heavy hearts.

In the middle of the night, when the house was quiet and pale moonlight shone into the workshop, two elves appeared. They were dressed in rags but had eyes as bright as buttons. They explored the workshop, balancing on balls of thread and peering into cupboards. Soon they found the leather and they set to work at once, snipping and sewing. As they worked, they sang:

"Busy little elves are we,
Working by the pale moonlight.
While the humans are asleep,
We are busy through the night!"

By dawn, the little elves had finished their work and disappeared.

When the shoemaker came to start work the next morning, he could not believe his eyes. There, on his workbench, was the finest pair of shoes he had ever seen.

"The stitches are so delicate," he said, as he showed his astonished wife the beautiful shoes. "I will place them in my window for everyone to see."

Soon a rich gentleman walked by the shop. He saw the stylish shoes and came inside. The rich gentleman tried on the shoes and they fit perfectly. He was so delighted that he gave the shoemaker twice the asking price.

"I can buy more leather!" said the shoemaker to his wife.

"But who could be helping us?" she replied.

That evening, the shoemaker cut out the leather for two pairs of shoes and left it on his workbench for the next morning.

In the middle of the night, the two elves appeared. They climbed on tools and swung from shoelaces. Soon they found the leather and set to work, snipping and sewing. As they worked, they sang:

"Busy little elves are we,
Working by the pale moonlight.
While the humans are asleep,
We are busy through the night!"

By dawn, the elves had finished their work and disappeared.

Once again, the shoemaker came into his workshop and found the shoes, neatly finished on his bench. The shoemaker placed them in his window. By now, the rich gentleman had told his friends about the shoemaker's fine work.

The two pairs of shoes sold that same day for more money than the shoemaker could ever have dreamed of.

That evening, the shoemaker cut out the leather for four more pairs of shoes. Then, the shoemaker and his wife hid and waited.

In the middle of the night, they watched in amazement as the two elves appeared. They danced with ribbons and juggled beads. Soon they found the leather and set to work, snipping and sewing. As they worked, they sang:

> *"Busy little elves are we,*
> *Working by the pale moonlight.*
> *While the humans are asleep,*
> *We are busy through the night!"*

"We must repay our little helpers for their kindness," said the shoemaker to his wife. "But how?"

"They were both dressed in rags," said the shoemaker's wife. "Why don't we make them some fine new clothes?"

"That's a wonderful idea!" said the shoemaker.

Although they were now very busy in their shop, the shoemaker and his wife spent every spare moment they had making their gift for the elves. They cut out fine cloth and leather, and sewed tiny seams. They crafted miniature buttons and knitted with toothpicks.

At last they had made two little pairs of trousers, two smart coats, two sturdy pairs of boots, and two warm, woolly scarves.

They wrapped the little outfits in paper and left them on the workbench for the elves to find.

That night, when the house was quiet and pale moonlight shone into the workshop, the shoemaker and his wife hid and waited. They watched happily as the two little elves appeared.

As usual, the elves explored the workshop. They made a tightrope from thread and bounced on a pincushion. Soon they found the tiny little outfits. They were delighted! They put on the trousers, the coats, the boots, and the scarves and danced merrily around the room.

As they danced, they sang:
"Busy little elves are we,
Working by the pale moonlight.
While the humans are asleep,
We are busy through the night!"

And then, the smart little elves put on their hats and
disappeared.

The shoemaker and his wife never saw the little elves again.
But the couple continued to make fine shoes for their shop and,
from that day on, they always prospered.

The Pied Piper

There was once a busy little town called Hamelin. The people of Hamelin lived happily, but there was one problem … the rats! There were rats in the cellars and rats in the rafters. The town's cats couldn't catch the rats, and the town's dogs couldn't fight the rats. Every day more and more rats scurried through the streets.

One day a stranger came to town. He was tall and thin like a birch tree and was dressed in bright fabric with a sweeping cape. He called himself the Pied Piper and around his neck he carried a long wooden pipe.

"I'll get rid of these rats for you, no problem!" he told the townspeople who had gathered around to greet him. "For a price, of course."

"There will be a sack of gold coins waiting if you succeed," promised the mayor.

The Pied Piper raised his pipe to his lips and began to play a mysterious tune. At first nothing happened, but then, one by one, rats started to appear. They came out of the doorways and the passageways. One peeked out from a loaf of bread and another from under the long skirts of a lady. They all scuttled over to where the piper played.

He danced and piped his way through the streets, and when he'd reached the town gates, he was followed by hundreds of rats. The people of Hamelin rang the church bells to celebrate as he lead the rats away from their homes for good.

Later that day, the Pied Piper came back for his gold coins, but the mayor only laughed.

"So much gold for one little tune. Do you think I'm a fool?" he chuckled and he tossed the Pied Piper just one gold coin.

The Pied Piper didn't say a word, but once again, he raised his pipe to his mouth. This time the tune was different, but it was so beautiful that everyone stopped to listen.

For a few moments the town was still, and the only sound was the pipe. But then there was a new sound … it was the sound of small feet pattering on the cobbles and, a moment later, all the children came running out to hear the music.

As the Pied Piper danced out of the gates, he was followed by every little child in the town. The townspeople could do nothing to stop the children as they ran laughing and skipping behind the piper, through the gates and far away.

No one knows how the story of Hamelin ended. Some say that once the mayor gave the Pied Piper the gold he had been promised, the children returned in the blink of an eye … but others say that that was the last time the people of Hamelin ever saw the Pied Piper or their children again.

The Princess and the Pea

Once upon a time, a king and queen lived in a castle with their only son, the prince. The couple were old, and they knew the prince would soon need to take up the throne.

But before he became king, the prince wanted to find a true princess to be his wife.

"Our son is handsome, brave, and clever," said the queen. "Yet the years rush past with no sound of wedding bells."

The king and queen sent the prince to travel the world in search of a princess he could love. He visited royal court after royal court, but eventually he returned home alone.

"I searched everywhere but couldn't find a true princess," said the prince. "I cannot marry anyone else. I am sorry."

So the prince gave up his search for a wife, and the king and queen continued to rule the kingdom.

Then one day, huge dark clouds stole over the valley. Thunder rumbled in the distance and rain lashed down. A chill breeze whistled around the castle. By nightfall it had spun itself into a terrible storm.

"Come and sit where it's warm," said the queen from the fire.

But as the prince took his seat, three faint knocks could just be heard above the noise of the storm. The prince helped his father pull open the castle's great oak doors. To their astonishment, a girl was standing outside.

"Good evening," she said politely. "May I please come in?"

The prince was taken aback as he looked at the stranger. She looked so beautiful standing there, even though she shivered in the cold night air.

"What are you doing out in this storm, child?" said the king.

"I was traveling when I lost my way," replied the girl. "I saw your castle and hoped you might allow me to stay here for the night. I am a princess, you see."

"Please," said the prince, reaching for the princess's hand, "let me show you inside."

"Thank you for your kindness," said the princess, curtseying.

The prince felt his cheeks flush. Something about this visitor made his heart tingle.

"Her clothes are simple and plain," whispered the king. "And yet she claims to be a princess. Can that really be true?"

The queen smiled knowingly. "Leave this to me," she replied. "I was a princess once and I know the perfect test. By morning we shall know the truth."

Over the next few hours the prince felt as if he could never tire of the princess's company. She had all the qualities of a true princess—she was kind, clever, funny, and thoughtful.

Meanwhile, the queen lit a fire in the guest bedroom and fetched soft blankets and towels.

"Your bedchamber is ready for you," said the queen at last. "Come this way."

The princess followed the queen up a winding staircase. At the very top was a candlelit room filled with an immense four-poster bed. The princess gasped. There had to be at least twenty mattresses piled onto the bed, stacked up in a dizzying tower!

"I do hope that you will be comfortable," said the queen, pointing to the giant bed. "We don't often have princesses stay at the castle."

The princess rubbed her eyes. "Thank you, Your Majesty," she said. "I am exhausted!"

The queen chuckled quietly to herself as she closed the princess's door. The visitor couldn't know what else the queen had prepared for her. At the very bottom of the bed, the queen had placed a single, tiny green pea.

"Sleep well, fair stranger," she mused. "Let's see if you are a true princess."

The king, queen, and prince were eating their breakfast when the princess appeared the next morning.

"Good morning," said the prince. "Please join us."

The princess stifled a yawn. She looked just as lovely as she had the night before, but her face seemed pale. There were dark shadows under her eyes.

"How did you sleep?" asked the king.

The princess looked at her lap. "There was a hard lump in my bed," she finally admitted. "I'm bruised black and blue from it. You've been so kind, but I couldn't sleep a wink."

The prince frowned with concern. But the queen had heard everything that she had hoped for. Much to the princess's surprise, she hugged her tightly.

"We have found our real princess!" she beamed. "Only a *true* princess would be delicate enough to feel a tiny pea through so many mattresses. Your precious bride has come to you at last, son!"

The prince had loved the princess from the moment he'd opened the castle door and seen her shivering in the rain.

"Would you do me the honor of marrying me?" he asked.

The princess's eyes sparkled with happiness. "Yes," she said.

The king and queen could rejoice at last. There was going to be a royal wedding!

The prince married his bride that very day. Every man, woman, and child in the kingdom joined in the celebrations, and church bells rang out. The newlyweds stood arm in arm on the castle ramparts, waving to the people below. The king and queen could rest at last, for the prince and his real princess were destined to live happily ever after.

This tale is true, but it happened a long time ago. If you are passing by the castle, be sure to visit its museum. There is a very special exhibit on display right at the back, in a dusty glass case. Peek inside and you'll see the proof of a *true* princess—a tiny, shrivelled pea.

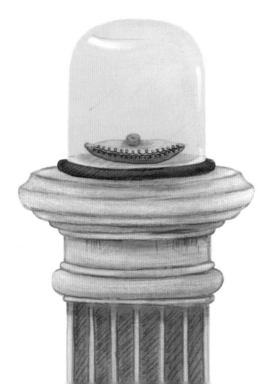

The Enormous Turnip

It was a bright spring morning and Jake was in the field with his dad. He gazed at the smooth, round seed in the palm of his father's hand.

"Eight weeks from now we'll have our first turnip harvest," his dad told him, tipping the last seed into the soil. He covered them with earth and Jake used his watering can to give the seeds a drink. Then the two of them strolled back to the farmhouse.

Spring turned into summer. Birds sang, flowers bloomed, and the turnips began to grow.

Jake watered them every day, and each time he returned the turnips had grown bigger.

But one of the turnips grew faster than any of the others.
So fast that one day, when Jake and his dad walked out to the field,
the enormous turnip towered over them both. It was certainly ready
for harvesting!

"What a turnip stew this beauty will make," said Dad. He
grasped the turnip by the base of the leaves and pulled. He heaved
until his face turned red, then at last staggered back and—**oof!**—fell
in a panting heap.

The turnip was still in the ground.

"Go and fetch your mother," Dad told Jake, who was trying not to laugh.

When Jake's mother arrived she held on to his father's suspenders, who in turn held on to the turnip. "Pull!" Jake called.

They heaved and pulled and strained, until at last they staggered back—**oof!**—into an apple tree.

"Come and help!" Jake's mother told him.

Jake's dad held on to the turnip. His wife held on to his suspenders. Jake held on to his mother's waist.

They heaved and pulled and strained and yanked until at last they collapsed—**oof!**—in a tangle of limbs.

As they helped each other up, the barn cat watched them. Jake looked up hopefully at his father.

"Okay, Misty can help, too," he grumbled.

Jake's dad held on to the turnip. His wife held on to his suspenders. Jake held on to his mother's waist. Misty held the hem of Jake's trousers between her teeth, and a little mouse scurried over to grasp Misty's tail.

All five of them heaved, and pulled, and strained, and yanked and—finally!—the turnip's white roots tore from the ground. The enormous vegetable rolled across the field and they chased after it.

"We did it!" Jake cried. Misty meowed triumphantly.

As they rolled the turnip back toward the farmhouse, Jake could already taste that evening's turnip stew. His mouth watered.

"All we had to do was work together," he said.

"You're right," his father told him. "But next year, let's grow peas instead."

Rapunzel

Once upon a time, a young couple lived in a cottage beside a stone wall. Although they were very poor, they were happy since the woman was expecting a baby.

On the other side of the wall lived an old witch. The witch grew many herbs and vegetables in her garden, but she kept them all for herself.

One day the couple had only a few potatoes to eat for their supper. They thought of the wonderful vegetable patch on the other side of the wall. It was full of delicious-looking carrots, cabbages, and tomatoes.

"Surely it wouldn't matter if we took just a few vegetables," said the wife, gazing longingly over the wall.

"We could make such good soup," agreed her husband.

So the young man quickly climbed over the wall and started to fill his basket with vegetables. Suddenly he heard an angry voice.

"How dare you steal my vegetables!" It was the witch.

"Please don't hurt me," begged the young man. "My wife is going to have a baby soon!"

"You may keep the vegetables—and your life," said the witch. "But you must give me the baby when it is born." Terrified, the man had no choice but to agree.

Months later, the woman gave birth to a little girl. Immediately, the witch arrived and grabbed the child. Though the parents begged and cried, the cruel witch took the baby. She called her Rapunzel.

Years passed and Rapunzel grew up to be kind and beautiful. The witch was so afraid of losing her that she built a tall tower with no door and only one window. She planted thorn bushes all around it, then she locked Rapunzel in the tower alone.

Each day, Rapunzel brushed her long, golden locks. And each day the witch came to visit her, standing at the foot of the tower and calling out, "Rapunzel, Rapunzel, let down your hair."

Rapunzel hung her hair out the window and the witch climbed up it to talk with her.

But Rapunzel was very lonely. She longed to leave the tower and to make friends her own age. Each day, she sat at her window and sang sadly.

One day, a young prince rode by and heard beautiful singing coming from the witch's garden. He hid behind a thorn bush, hoping to see the singer. But instead he saw the witch. He watched as she stood below the tower and called, "Rapunzel, Rapunzel, let down your hair."

The prince saw the cascade of golden hair fall from the window and he watched the witch climb up it.

He waited until the witch climbed back down the hair and returned to her house. Rapunzel began her song again.

Enchanted by Rapunzel's lovely voice, the prince climbed over the wall, battled through the thorns, and creeped to the tower.

"Rapunzel, Rapunzel, let down your hair," he called softly.

Rapunzel let down her locks and the prince climbed up.

Poor Rapunzel was terribly afraid—she had never seen anyone except the witch before. But when the prince explained that he only wanted to be her friend, Rapunzel was delighted.

From then on, the prince visited her every day. Each time, he carefully waited until after the witch had left before calling to Rapunzel to let down her hair.

Months passed and Rapunzel and the prince fell in love.

"How can we be together?" Rapunzel cried. "The witch will never let me go."

The prince had an idea. He brought silk, which Rapunzel knotted together to make a ladder so that she could escape from the tower when the time was right.

One day, without thinking, Rapunzel remarked to the witch, "It's much harder to pull you up than the prince!"

"Prince?" shouted the witch. "What prince?"

Furious, the witch grabbed Rapunzel's long hair and cut it off. Then she used her magic to send Rapunzel far into the forest.

Soon, the prince came to the tower and called, "Rapunzel, Rapunzel, let down your hair."

The witch held the golden hair out of the window and the prince climbed up and into the tower. But instead of Rapunzel, he came face to face with the ugly old witch.

"You dare to visit Rapunzel?" said the witch. "You will never see her again!"

And she pushed the prince back out of the window. He fell down and down, right into the thorn bushes below. The sharp spikes scratched the prince's eyes and blinded him.

After months of wandering, blind and lost, the prince
heard beautiful, sad singing floating through the woods.
He recognized Rapunzel's voice immediately and called out to her.

Rapunzel ran to the prince and held him in her arms.

"At last, I have found you!" she said, and cried with happiness.
As her tears fell onto his injured eyes, the wounds healed and
the prince could see again.

"My love!" he said and kissed Rapunzel.

Rapunzel had never been so happy. She and the prince
returned to his kingdom. They were soon married, and Rapunzel's
parents came to the wedding, delighted to be reunited
with their daughter.

Rapunzel and the prince lived happily
ever after in a grand castle, far
away from the old witch and
her empty tower.

The Miller, His Son, and the Donkey

Once there was a miller who had a young son and an old donkey. The miller was very poor, and one day he decided that he would sell the donkey. It was old and gray, but it would still fetch a good price at market. As soon as the sun rose, they set off, the miller striding in front, the donkey trotting beside him, and the miller's son skipping along behind them.

It was a bright sunny morning, and because it was market day, the road was full of people walking to the town or back home. The miller's neighbor was one of them, and he stopped to say hello.

"It's a fine day for a walk, my friend, but why don't one of you ride on your donkey? The market is still far from here. Take my advice: you'll all be walking for hours if you don't."

"What a good idea!" said the miller gratefully. "We'll get there much quicker if we do as you say."

With that, he helped his son onto the donkey's back, and they set off along the road again, the miller striding in front and his son on the donkey, who was walking along behind.

The road passed between two fields, one of which was full of farmworkers cutting corn. As the miller came along, two of the workers stopped what they were doing and called out, "Your donkey looks strong enough to carry you, Mr. Miller. Why don't you ride on it instead of your son? Take a break, or you will be too tired for the full walk!"

"That's a great idea!" replied the miller happily. "When I've sold the donkey, I'll have no choice except to walk everywhere, but today, I can ride."

With that, he took his son's place on the donkey, and they all set off once more, the donkey plodding along, the miller riding, and the miller's son jogging beside them.

After a little while, they came to a broad river, where a group of young women were washing their clothes in the water. As the miller passed by, one of them looked up at him and cried, "You should be ashamed of yourself, Mr. Miller! You're riding on the donkey while your little boy has to run to keep up!"

The miller's face turned red with shame. "You're right," he said. "It was thoughtless of me. After all, there's room on the donkey for both of us. Thank you." The miller lifted up his son to sit in front of him, and they all set off once more, the donkey plodding along slowly with the man and the boy on his back.

They were nearly to the town now, which was just as well, because the donkey was starting to struggle under the weight of the miller and his son.

A townsman who was walking past them saw the donkey stumble and frowned at the miller.

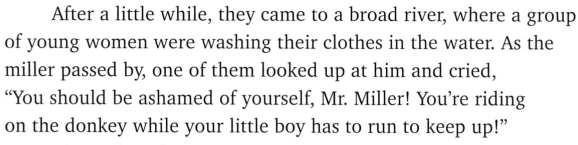

"Your donkey is exhausted, poor thing. You and your son should be carrying it, instead of it carrying you!"

"Oh yes," said the miller, looking guilty. "I was being thoughtless again. We'll take your advice, sir, and thank you for it."

With that, he and his son jumped off the donkey and chopped down a tall, slender tree. They used this as a pole and tied the donkey to it by its hooves. Then they hoisted the pole onto their shoulders and carried the donkey into the marketplace.

When the miller and his son reached the market, the stall owners fell over laughing.

"Just look at that!" cried one woman, tears of laughter rolling down her cheeks. "That donkey must be very special to be carried to market on a pole. Be careful that you don't let its hooves touch the dirty ground, Mr. Miller!"

The miller felt very silly indeed. He felt even sillier when the donkey, who was tired of being jiggled along on the pole, kicked out with all four legs together, snapped the ropes that held it to the pole, and fell to the ground.

The donkey ran off back down the road and into the open countryside, free at last.

The miller and his son stood there, open mouthed, and watched it disappear. All they could do now was go back home with no money, no donkey, and very red faces.

Thumbelina

There was once a poor woman who lived in a cottage. She had no husband, but she longed to have a child. One day, she visited a fairy to ask for her help.

"You are a good woman," said the fairy, "so I will give you this magic seed. Plant it and water it, and you will see what you will see."

The woman thanked the fairy and did as she was told. Three days passed, and nothing happened. But on the fourth day, a tiny green shoot appeared. And on the fifth day, there was a flower bud, with glossy pink petals wrapped tightly around its center.

"What a beautiful flower you will be," smiled the woman, and she kissed it gently.

With that, the petals unfolded, and in the center of the flower was a beautiful girl, the size of a thumb. The woman clapped her hands with joy.

"I will call you Thumbelina," she cried. She laid her new child in a walnut-shell bed with a rose-petal quilt.

Thumbelina was very happy with her mother.

Then one day while her mother was away, an ugly, slimy toad crawled into the cottage.

When she saw Thumbelina sleeping in the bed, she cried, "You'd be the perfect wife for my son!" She grabbed the girl and creeped out of the cottage.

When Thumbelina woke up, she was sitting on a lily pad in the middle of a stream, with two warty toads staring at her.

"This is your new wife!" the mother said to her son.

He opened his wide, toothless mouth in a grin, but all he could say was, "Croak! Croak!"

"I don't want to marry a toad," said Thumbelina, and she started to cry.

"How ungrateful," the mother toad scolded. "You'll stay here until you stop crying." The two toads jumped into the water and swam away.

Thumbelina sobbed and sobbed. After an hour or so, a passing fish took pity on her and nibbled through the lily pad's stem until it floated free.

"Thank you!" called Thumbelina, as she sailed downstream.

At last, she drifted to the riverbank and climbed onto dry land. Suddenly, a big brown beetle grabbed her with its claws.

"Put me down!" said Thumbelina.

"No," said the beetle. "You must marry me."

The beetle carried Thumbelina to a clearing. Another bigger beetle was waiting for him there. He looked at Thumbelina and shook his head.

"Oh, Bertie, she's so ugly," said the bigger beetle. "If you marry her, everyone will laugh at you!"

The two beetles argued, waving their claws in the air and pulling poor Thumbelina this way and that, until at last they let Thumbelina go. She ran off as fast as she could.

Thumbelina lived in the country all summer long. She missed her mother, but had no idea how to find her way home. So she busied herself collecting wild berries and making friends with the birds and small creatures she met.

When winter came, Thumbelina was cold and hungry until a kind field mouse invited her to stay with him in his burrow. She was so grateful that she said yes at once.

Life underground was warm and snug, but Thumbelina soon missed the sunshine. And then Mouse's friend Mole asked her to marry him.

"I don't want to marry a mole," cried Thumbelina. "And though I like living with you, Mouse, I miss the sunshine."

"You ungrateful girl!" said the mouse and the mole together. So Thumbelina sadly agreed to marry the mole and a date was set for the following summer.

Thumbelina was miserable. Then one day, as she walked through the underground tunnels, she found a swallow, almost dead with the cold. She hugged the bird against herself to warm him.

The bird's heartbeat grew stronger. He slowly opened his eyes. "You have saved my life," said the swallow. "I flew into a storm while I was traveling South, to the land of sunshine and flowers. Come with me?"

"I cannot leave Mouse," sighed Thumbelina, "he has been so kind to me. And I have promised to marry Mole."

"Do you want to marry this mole?" asked the swallow.

"Well … no," admitted Thumbelina.

"Then it is settled," said the swallow, stretching his wings. "Come on!"

"I will!" said Thumbelina.

So Thumbelina flew away to the South with the swallow. As she explored her new home, one especially beautiful flower opened in front of her. There, in the center, was a fairy prince, no bigger than a thumb.

"Will you be my wife?" he asked at once.

"I will!" cried Thumbelina.

So Thumbelina, wearing butterfly wings made especially for her, married the prince and became Queen of the Flower Fairies.

She did not forget her mother, and that very day arranged for fairy messengers to deliver a letter to her and a bouquet of the most beautiful flowers.

Kind Thumbelina and her handsome husband lived happily ever after.

Stone Soup

Once upon a time, a hungry traveler arrived at a small village. He knocked on the door of the first house he came to.

"Excuse me, sir," the traveler said when a man answered the door. "Could you spare a scrap of food?"

"No, I can't," the man replied. "I only have enough food for myself. Don't bother me again."

The traveler knocked on many more doors, but each villager said that they barely had food enough for themselves. Finally, the traveler passed a little girl playing in her garden.

"Hello there," said the traveler. "Everyone in this village must be so hungry. If only I could find a pot and some firewood, I would be able to make my delicious stone soup for us all to share."

"You can't make soup from a stone!" said the girl.

"Of course you can!" replied the traveler. "Have you never tried stone soup? How sad. It's the most delicious soup in the world."

"I'd like to try it," said the girl. "Wait here."

Soon she returned dragging a big copper pot and a bundle of firewood.

The traveler built a fire and placed the pot on top.

Then he carefully opened a bundle of purple silk and lifted out a big, round stone. He placed it in the bottom of the pot.

"Now we need water. Could we take some from your well?" asked the traveler.

"Come with me," said the girl, and together they filled the big pot with water. Then they sat down to wait. Just as the pot began to bubble, the girl's father approached.

"We're making stone soup," said the girl. "It's the most delicious soup in the world!"

"I've never heard of it," said her father. "Is it ready?"

"Nearly," said the traveler, "but it is a shame there are no carrots or potatoes. They make stone soup even more tasty."

"Why, I have a couple of carrots," said the father. "And one of my neighbors might have a potato or two."

He sent his daughter to fetch the neighbors and soon there were carrots and potatoes in the soup.

"It won't be quite as delicious as usual without the traditional meat or seasoning," said the traveler. "But not to worry!"

"We have meat," said one of the villagers quickly.

"And I have salt and spices," said another.

Soon there were chunks of juicy meat in the stone soup. The traveler added salt and spices and stirred the pot five times.

"The soup is ready," he said. "Everyone bring a bowl!"

The whole village enjoyed the stone soup, which was just as delicious as the traveler had promised.

When the last of the soup had been mopped up, the traveler lifted the stone out of the empty pot and wrapped it in the purple silk. Many of the villagers asked to buy the stone but he refused.

"This stone is worth more than gold and riches," he told them. As the traveler made his way out of the village, he passed the girl.

"Here," he said handing her the bundle of purple silk. "Now you will always be able to make stone soup for everyone who's hungry."

Cinderella

Once upon a time, there was a young girl who lived with her father, stepmother, and two stepsisters. The stepmother was jealous of the girl, and when the father died she became spiteful.

Soon the young girl was made to do all the housework, eat scraps, and sleep by the fireplace. Because she slept in the ashes and cinders, they began to call her "Cinderella."

One day, a letter arrived from the palace. All the women in the land were invited to attend a grand ball—where the prince would choose a bride!

Cinderella's stepsisters were very excited. Her stepmother was sure one of her daughters would marry the prince, and made Cinderella work night and day to make them as beautiful as possible.

Dear all women in the land, (yes, you) The prince requests the honor of your company at a ball. Everyone welcome. Dress to impress.

Cinderella washed and curled their dull hair. She cut and shaped their ragged nails. She stitched their ballgowns and she polished their dancing shoes until they shone.

Cinderella longed to go to the ball herself, but her stepsisters just laughed.

"You? Go to a ball?" the elder stepsister said. "But you don't have a gown!"

"You? Go to a ball?" laughed the younger stepsister. "But you are covered in soot and cinders!"

Tears ran down Cinderella's soot-stained face as she helped her stepsisters into their dresses and jewels. At last they left for the ball, and Cinderella sat alone by the fireplace. She cried and cried.

"If only I could be happy for one night," she said through her tears. "I so wish I could go to the ball."

Cinderella had barely finished speaking when a sparkle of light appeared in the dull kitchen. It was a fairy!

"You *shall* go to the ball!" the fairy said. "I am your fairy godmother, and I will make it so."

Cinderella stared in amazement at the fairy. Quickly, she dried her eyes. "Really? Can I really go to the ball?" she asked, barely daring to believe it.

"Yes, my dear. You just need a spot of magic to help you on your way," the fairy answered.

The fairy godmother told her to find a pumpkin, four white mice, and a black rat. Cinderella hurried to the garden for a pumpkin. She found four mice in the kitchen, and she caught a rat sleeping in the barn. She hurried back with them to the fairy godmother.

With a wave of the fairy's wand, the pumpkin turned into a gleaming golden coach.

Cinderella gasped in astonishment. "It's beautiful!" she said. "But who will drive it?"

The fairy waved her wand again, and the four mice became four handsome white horses. She waved her wand a third time and the rat turned into a tall coachman.

"How wonderful!" Cinderella cried. But then she caught sight of her reflection in the gleaming carriage. "Oh … I can't go to the ball in these rags."

"And you won't go in rags," said her fairy godmother.

Again she waved her magic wand and Cinderella's rags turned into a shimmering ballgown. Glittering glass slippers appeared on her feet. Cinderella looked beautiful.

"Now, off you go," the fairy godmother said, "but be warned; the magic will wear off at midnight, so make sure you are home."

Cinderella climbed into the coach, and it whisked her away to the palace.

She had never been happier.

When Cinderella arrived at the royal ball everyone was captivated, wondering who the lovely stranger could be.

The prince himself immediately asked Cinderella to dance, and was so enchanted with her that he danced with no one else all evening. They whirled and twirled on the glittering dance floor for hours.

Cinderella enjoyed herself so much that she completely forgot her fairy godmother's warning.

Suddenly, the palace clock began to strike midnight.

Cinderella picked up her skirts and fled. The worried prince ran after her as she raced down the palace steps.

She lost one of her glass slippers on the way, but she didn't stop. She jumped into the the waiting coach, and drove off before the prince could stop her.

On the final stroke of midnight, Cinderella found herself sitting on the road beside a pumpkin. Four white mice and a black rat scampered around her. She was dressed in rags and had only a single glass slipper left from her magical evening.

"Even if it was a dream," she said to herself, "it was a perfect dream."

At the palace, the prince looked longingly at the glass slipper he had found on the steps. He could not forget the wonderful girl he had danced with all night.

"I will find her," he said, "and I will marry her!"

He took the glass slipper and set out to visit every house in the land, asking every single maiden to try on the slipper.

At last he came to Cinderella's house, where her stepsisters tried to squeeze their huge feet into the delicate slipper. But no matter what they did, they could not get it to fit.

Cinderella had been scrubbing the courtyard, and she gasped when she saw the prince and the glittering glass shoe. "My slipper!" she cried.

"You didn't even go to the ball!" laughed the eldest stepsister.

"Everyone must try," the prince said. There was something familiar about this sooty serving girl.

Everyone watched as Cinderella's foot slid easily into the glass slipper. The prince took Cinderella in his arms at once.

"You're the one!" he said. "Will you do me the honor of marrying me?"

Cinderella's stepmother and stepsisters were furious. "It can't be her!" they cried.

Cinderella took the other slipper from her pocket. "Yes, it was me," Cinderella said, "and yes, I will marry you."

Much to the disgust of her stepmother and stepsisters, Cinderella married the prince the very next day and went to live in the palace. The couple lived long, happy lives together, and Cinderella's stepmother and her daughters had to do their own cleaning and never went to another ball at the palace.

The End

The Goose that Laid the Golden Egg

A poor farmer and his wife lived in a small stone cottage by a stream. All they owned in the world was the cottage, a little vegetable patch, a tired old cow, and one white goose.

Every day, they had milk from the cow for breakfast, cabbage from the vegetable patch for lunch, and a goose egg with toast for their dinner. The goose laid only one egg each day, so the farmer and his wife had to share it.

Early one morning, the farmer went out to collect the daily egg from the goose's nest. He reached under the bird, into the warm straw, and his fingers closed around something —but it didn't feel like a normal egg. For one thing, it was HUGE, and for another, it was HEAVY. In fact, the farmer struggled to lift the egg out of the nest, and when he held it up to look at it, he saw that it was golden.

"This egg looks like gold. It feels as heavy as gold, too," he gasped. "Could it be? The goose has laid a golden egg!" He rushed into the cottage to tell his wife.

"We're rich," she cried. "Yippee!"

The pair danced around the kitchen, knocking over the pot of boiled cabbage that was cooling on the table. They couldn't believe their good fortune.

The goose laid another egg the following day, a third egg the day after, and on and on for weeks. The weeks turned into months, and still the goose kept laying those fabulous golden eggs.

The farmer and his wife lost no time in spending their newfound wealth. They bought a huge mansion to live in, they rode everywhere in a smart carriage pulled by six fine horses, and they didn't eat milk for breakfast, cabbage for lunch, and an egg with toast for dinner anymore.

They ate only the finest foods prepared by a world-famous chef. They bought the goose a jeweled collar to wear and a red velvet cushion to sit on, which she liked a lot. It still laid only one egg a day, though.

Years passed, and the farmer and his wife got richer and richer. They had so much money that they didn't know what to spend it on. But that didn't stop them wanting even more.

One night, the farmer woke up suddenly and sat bolt upright in bed. He'd had a brilliant idea. It was such a good idea that he couldn't wait until morning to tell his wife. He woke her up.

"I know how we can get even more gold," he told her gleefully. "Our goose lays only one egg a day, doesn't she? But she must have more golden eggs inside her, waiting to come out. If we could get them out, think of all the money we would have!"

"I'm sure you're right, my love," replied his wife, giving him a big kiss on the cheek. "Let's get all those lovely eggs and spend all that lovely money as soon as we can!"

First thing the next morning, the farmer cut open the goose to find the golden eggs that he thought were inside her. He searched every inch of that goose, but, much to his disappointment, there were no more golden eggs in there.

In fact, after he had cut the goose open, there were no more golden eggs at all, ever.

Without their golden eggs, the farmer and his wife began to run out of money. It wasn't long before they had to sell the mansion and go to live in a stone cottage again. They had to sell the carriage, too, and send the chef away.

Soon, their lives were back to the way they had been before the goose started laying the golden eggs. They worked in the vegetable patch, milked the cow, ate cabbage and toast, with not even one egg to share between them.

In fact, their lives were worse than they were before, because the farmer and his wife couldn't forget how very silly they had been to be so greedy.

Jack and the Beanstalk

Once upon a time, there was a young boy called Jack, who lived with his mother in a cottage. They were so poor that, bit by bit, they had to sell everything they owned just to buy their food.

Then one day, Jack's mother said to him, "We will have to sell Bluebell, our old cow. Take her to the market, Jack, and remember to sell her for a good price."

So Jack took Bluebell off to market. He had just reached the edge of the town when an old man appeared at the side of the road.

"Are you going to sell that fine cow?" said the man.

"Yes," said Jack.

"Well, I'll buy her from you, and I'll give you these magic beans," said the man, holding out a handful of dry beans. "I know they don't look like much, but if you plant them, you will be rich beyond your wildest dreams."

Jack liked the sound of being rich … "It's a deal!" he said, shaking the stranger's hand at once. He gave Bluebell to the man and took the beans. Wouldn't his mother be pleased!

When Jack showed his mother the beans, she was so angry that her face turned as red as a beet!

"You stupid boy! Go to your room!" she cried, and threw the beans out of the window.

Jack sat on his bed, feeling miserable. "Stupid beans," he muttered. "Stupid me!" Then he fell asleep.

When Jack woke up the next morning, it was strangely dark in his room and all he could see through the window were the leaves of a huge plant—a plant so tall that he couldn't see the top of it.

"It's a beanstalk!" cried Jack. "What's at the top?"

Jack started to climb. Up he went, from branch to branch and from leaf to leaf. At the top was a giant house.

Jack's tummy was rumbling with hunger, so he knocked on the great big door. A giant woman answered.

"Please, ma'am, may I have some breakfast?" Jack asked politely.

"You'll become breakfast if my husband finds you!" said the giant's wife.

Jack begged and pleaded and at last she let him in and gave him some bread and milk.

The giant's wife had just shown Jack where to hide when the giant came home in a bad mood.

"Fee, fi, fo, fum, I smell the blood of an Englishman!" he roared.

"It's just the sausages I have cooked you," laughed his wife.

The giant ate a giant-sized breakfast, then sat down to count the huge gold coins in his treasure chest.

"One hundred and one … one hundred and two …" he counted, but his head started to nod and before long he was fast asleep.

Quick as a flash, Jack grabbed one of the huge gold coins. He raced to the beanstalk and climbed down it as fast as his legs would carry him.

His mother was so happy to see the gold that she hugged Jack for ten whole minutes!

"We'll never be poor again!" she laughed.

Before long, however, Jack and his mother had spent all the money, so the boy decided to climb the beanstalk again.

As before, Jack knocked on the door and asked the giant's wife for some food.

She gave him some bread and milk and hid him in the cupboard just as the giant arrived home.

When the giant had eaten a giant-sized lunch, his wife brought him his golden goose. "Lay!" he said, and the goose laid a solid gold egg. It laid ten eggs before the giant started to snore.

Jack could hardly believe his luck! Quick as a flash, he picked up the goose and ran.

Although Jack and his mother were now rich beyond their wildest dreams, Jack decided to climb the beanstalk one more time.

This time, Jack sneaked in when the giant's wife wasn't looking and quickly hid in the cupboard.

The giant came home as usual and ate a giant-sized dinner, then his wife brought him his magic harp.

"Play!" he roared, and the harp began to play. It was such sweet music that the giant fell asleep in record time!

Jack grabbed the harp and started to run, but the giant woke up at once and chased after him!

The boy slithered down the beanstalk faster than he'd ever done before. "Mother, quick, fetch me the ax!" Jack yelled as he reached the ground. He chopped at the beanstalk with all his might.

Creak! Groan!

The giant quickly climbed back up to the top just before the beanstalk crashed to the ground.

Jack never saw the giant again. He, his mother, and the golden goose lived happily ever after.

The Wind and the Sun

One sunny but cold fall day, the Sun shone down on the earth below and sighed happily.

She could see people strolling down streets or working outside, children playing in parks, boats sailing on sparkling water, cows and sheep grazing in fields, and birds sitting in the trees, cheerily singing their merry songs.

"What a wonderful sight," said the Sun, as she shone brightly. "I will certainly enjoy my journey across the sky today."

As she gazed across the clear sky, a sudden burst of cold air blew across her face and sent clouds scurrying along her path.

"Out of my way!" growled the Wind, racing past the Sun. "No time to waste. I have work to do!"

"What are you up to?" the Sun called out.

"See those trees down there? I'm going to blow all the leaves off!" roared the Wind.

He blew so hard that the branches of the trees were left bare, and the birds stood shivering. They weren't singing their happy tunes anymore.

"Why do you have to cause such misery all the time?" asked the Sun. "Now birds have nowhere to shelter, and people are rushing into their houses."

But the Wind just laughed. "I like showing how strong I am. You might be happy to just sit around in the sky all day, but I need to use up all my energy and strength."

The Sun looked at the Wind and smiled to herself.

"Why don't we have a contest to see which of us is stronger," said the Sun.

"Ha! It will be a waste of time," cackled the boastful Wind.

"Let's just wait and see," replied the Sun. "See that man down there? Whoever can get him to remove his coat is the strongest. Agreed?"

The Wind looked down at the man, who was strolling through a park. Since it was a cold day, he had on a heavy coat to keep him warm.

"Agreed," chuckled the Wind. "This will be easy."

"Go on, then," said the Sun. "I'll hide behind a cloud to keep out of your way."

The Wind, happy to show off again, puffed himself up to his full size and blew and blew. He blew so hard that the fallen leaves swirled around the park, and the poor birds were nearly blown off the branches as they huddled together for warmth.

The man pulled up the collar of his coat around his ears. The Wind blew and blew some more. The birds gave up their struggle and flew off to find somewhere else to shelter. The man pulled up his hood and tightened his scarf around his neck.

The Sun watched from behind the cloud and grinned to herself, as the Wind blew harder and harder and grew more and more furious.

The harder he blew, the tighter the man pulled his coat around his body. The Wind tore angrily at the coat, but all his efforts were in vain.

At last, after one huge and final puff, the Wind called out to the Sun, "My puff is all gone! I need to rest."

The Sun came out from behind the cloud. "All right, I'll take my turn now."

The Wind watched as the Sun began to shine. At first, her rays were gentle. Slowly, the cold air began to warm up. The swirling leaves settled on the ground, and the birds flew back down to perch in the branches of the trees.

The man stopped walking and looked around. It was very pleasant to feel the warmth of the Sun's rays on his face.

The Sun shone a little brighter. The man loosened his scarf and pulled down his hood. The Sun breathed in the last of the cold air and sent down more warm rays. The man unbuttoned his coat.

Finally, as the Sun's rays grew warmer and warmer, the man took off his coat and sat under a tree.

"I think I will take a rest to enjoy this lovely, unexpected heat," sighed the man happily.

The Wind couldn't believe it. He huffed angrily in defeat.

"Your freezing blasts of air just made the man more determined to keep his coat on," said the Sun. "But my gentle rays made him feel warm, so he no longer needed his coat to protect him from the cold. And look how happy he is now!"

The Wind sighed. He had learned a valuable lesson. Gentleness and kindness are more persuasive than force and bluster.

The Sorcerer's Apprentice

Once upon a time, a young boy called Franz went to work as an apprentice for a sorcerer. The sorcerer lived in a castle overlooking the little village where Franz lived with his family. It was considered a great honor to help and learn from such a clever and powerful man.

Franz was very excited about learning how to do magic. But when he arrived on his first day, he was given a long list of chores to do around the castle—cleaning, tidying up, and fetching water from the well.

Franz was not happy. "It's not fair!" he muttered to himself. "I didn't come here to be his servant. When will I get to do some magic?"

The sorcerer was a busy man. Each morning he would tell his apprentice what chores needed doing that day. He would then disappear into his workshop in the castle or journey out to one of the surrounding villages in the area, leaving Franz alone.

Occasionally, as Franz went about the castle doing his chores, he would catch a glimpse of the great sorcerer looking through the pages of a large leather-bound book. The pages of this book were filled with beautiful illustrations and the words of the sorcerer's magic spells. Franz longed to have a look in the book himself, but the sorcerer kept it locked in a wooden cabinet in his workshop.

Several months later, fed up with doing chores all day, Franz decided he would sneak a look in the sorcerer's special spell book when the old man was gone.

As the sorcerer got ready to leave the castle that day, he called out to Franz.

"Boy, I need you to scrub the floor of the Great Hall for me," he said. "You will need to fetch water from the well with this bucket, and carry it to the big stone container in the hall."

Franz rolled his eyes behind the sorcerer's back. "Of course," he mumbled.

"When the container is full of water," continued the sorcerer, "take the broom and give the floor a good scrub. I want to see it shining when I get back this afternoon."

As soon as the sorcerer left, Franz climbed the small staircase to the workshop. He knew where the sorcerer kept the key to the wooden cabinet, so he grabbed it and hurriedly opened the old, creaking doors. Inside sat the magic spell book.

Franz carried the heavy book to the Great Hall and sat down to look through its magical pages. There were spells for all sorts of weird and wonderful things.

As he turned the pages, Franz saw a spell that could bring any object to life. This gave him a brilliant idea.

"What harm can one little spell do?" he thought to himself.

Grinning, Franz rushed to fetch the broom and bucket. He placed the broom on the floor, sat back down at the desk, and slowly chanted the words of the magic spell. He couldn't wait to see the broom clean the Great Hall by itself!

At first nothing happened. Franz was just about to try the spell
again, when suddenly the broom sprouted little arms and leaped up
from the floor. Franz was so surprised he nearly fell off his chair.

This was amazing. He was doing magic!

"Broom!" he commanded. "Take the bucket to the well and
fetch water to fill that container."

The broom marched off to the well and started carrying the
bucket backward and forward between the well and the container
in the Great Hall.

Franz couldn't believe his eyes. Laughing as the little broom
continued to bring the water, he cried, "I am the master! And you
must obey me!"

After a while, Franz noticed the container was overflowing and the water was running all over the floor.

"Stop, little broom!" he shouted. But the broom carried on fetching water.

Flipping through the pages of the magic book, Franz tried desperately to find a spell to make the broom stop. But the broom kept on going.

By now the water was all over the floor. Franz grabbed an ax and chopped the broom into small pieces.

"That should do it," he said with a sigh of relief.

But to his dismay, the little pieces of broom started to move and grow, and they too sprouted arms and legs. Soon there was an army of new brooms. They all marched to the well to fetch more water.

The brooms continued splashing the water into the Great Hall and soon it was swirling around Franz's knees. He was powerless to stop the brooms.

Just then, the sorcerer returned. He raised his arms and in a booming voice, chanted a magic spell. In an instant the brooms all vanished and the water disappeared.

Franz fell to his knees. "Please forgive me, master," he begged.

"I just wanted to try some magic."

"You should never play with things you don't understand," said the sorcerer. "Magic is very powerful."

Franz hung his head in shame. He would never get the chance to learn magic now.

"I should send you away, boy," continued the sorcerer. He could see that Franz was very sorry, and he hesitated.

"I suppose you can stay," he said. "You still have much training to complete."

"Thank you so much, sir," said Franz, relieved. "I promise I will work extra hard."

"Well," said the sorcerer, "you can start by cleaning this floor—the old-fashioned way!"

The Emperor's New Clothes

Once upon a time, there lived an emperor who loved clothes. He would strut around his palace in a parade of different outfits, day and night. There were mirrors in every room so he could admire his reflection as he passed by.

The emperor had comfy outfits for the morning, made from silk and trimmed in feathers.

He had stylish outfits for the afternoon, made from wool and dyed in rich colors.

And he had extra special outfits for the evening, made from the most expensive cloth and sewn with pure gold thread.

In fact, the emperor had so many clothes that he often didn't know what to wear!

One day, two wicked men called at the palace. They knew all about the emperor's love of clothes.

"Your Highness, we are weavers," they said. "But we can do something that no other weavers can do. We can make a magic cloth. This cloth is very special because only very clever people can see it."

The emperor was impressed. "I would like you to make me a suit from this magic cloth," he said.

"Of course, Your Highness, it would be an honor," said the first weaver.

They began to measure the emperor, who pouted and preened in the mirror, imagining himself in his new suit.

"Sire, we will need lots of gold thread," said the second weaver.

"You shall have all the gold thread you need," replied the emperor. He turned to one of his servants. "Please show these fine gentlemen to the royal storeroom."

The two men had never seen so much gold thread. Laughing and clapping their hands with glee, they filled their bags and left the palace.

A few days later the emperor called for one of his ministers. "Go and find out how the weavers are getting on," he ordered. "I need something new to wear."

The minister went off to the weavers' workshop. There he found the two weavers sitting in front of a loom, busy at work. The minister rubbed his eyes. He couldn't see any cloth.

"That's strange," he thought. Not wanting to appear foolish, he smiled at the weavers. "The cloth is looking wonderful. When will the emperor's suit be ready?" he asked.

"Soon, soon," replied the first weaver.

"But we will need more gold thread to complete the suit," said the second weaver.

The minister hurried back to the emperor.

As soon as he had gone, the weavers roared with laughter.

"Oh, this is priceless! What a foolish man!"

Back at the palace, the minister bowed before the emperor. Not wishing to be called a fool he said, "Sire, I have never seen a cloth more beautiful. The weavers need more gold thread to finish your suit."

"Well, send more over then," replied the emperor.

For a whole week the weavers pretended to cut and sew the magic cloth to make the new suit. At last they returned to the palace, proudly pretending to carry the cloth.

The emperor was very excited and handed the weavers a heavy bag of gold coins to pay for the outfit. He took off his clothes and the weavers fussed around him, pretending to smooth and adjust the new suit.

"It fits you perfectly!" they cried.

The emperor looked in the mirror. He couldn't see any clothes, but not wanting to appear foolish, he said, "It's wonderful!"

As soon as the two men had left the palace, they doubled over with laughter. Their plan had worked, and now they were rich!

News of the emperor's special new suit quickly spread throughout the kingdom. Everyone was sure they would be able to see the magic cloth.

"Yes, Sire, truly splendid!" agreed the emperor's ministers.

No matter how hard he looked, the emperor still could not see any clothes.

"I can't be more of a fool than my ministers," he thought, "and they can all see the suit." So he ordered them to send out a royal announcement. He would lead a grand procession through the city wearing his new suit.

When the great day arrived, people gathered in the streets to catch a glimpse of the emperor as the procession passed by.

Finally the emperor appeared riding on a fine white horse. Nervous whispers rippled through the crowd. No one wanted to appear foolish, so at last a timid voice called out, "The emperor's new clothes are magnificent!"

Suddenly everyone started talking and shouting at once.

"How stylish!"

"Smart and fashionable!"

The emperor smiled as he trotted along, feeling very pleased with himself.

Then a small boy and his sister pushed to the front of the crowd. They started to point and giggle.

"Look!" they cried. "The emperor has no clothes on!"

Suddenly, everyone realized that it was true. Before long the laughter had spread through the crowd in waves.

The emperor turned bright red.

"What a fool I am!" he gasped. "How could I have been so silly and vain?" He looked around for the two weavers, but of course they were nowhere to be seen.

Filled with shame, the emperor made his way back to the palace.

"I will never be so vain about my clothes again," said the emperor to his minister, as he was helped back into his old suit. "I promise that I'll start to be a better emperor and will spend less time looking in the mirror."

He was true to his word—and he was a much happier emperor from that day on.

The Moon in the Well

In a faraway place, at the foot of the mountains, there lived a rather silly man. One clear, moonlit night, the man woke up feeling thirsty so he went outside to draw water from the well.

He leaned over the rough, brick edge of the well and peered down into the water far below. As he did so, he let out a cry.

"What a disaster!" he shouted into the quiet of the night. "The moon has tumbled into the well."

The man's cries woke up his rather silly wife. She came running out of the house and joined her husband at the edge of the well. She peered down into the water far below.

"What a disaster! What a catastrophe!" she wailed. "The moon has tumbled into the well."

The wife's cries woke up their rather silly daughter. She came out of the house rubbing her eyes, and joined her parents at the edge of the well. She peered down into the water far below.

"What a disaster! What a catastrophe! What a calamity!" she cried. "The moon has tumbled into the well."

"We must hook it out," said her father firmly. He tied a hook to a long rope and lowered it into the well. As it splashed into the water, he began to pull the rope up again.

The side of the well was built with rough stones, and as the man pulled the rope the hook became caught on one of them. No matter how hard the silly man pulled, he just couldn't lift the hook.

"Wife, you must help me pull," called the silly man. "The moon is as heavy as you and I."

His silly wife pulled on the rope behind him, but they still couldn't lift the moon out of the well.

"Daughter, you must help us pull," called the silly wife. "The moon is as heavy as all three of us."

The silly daughter joined her silly parents and together they pulled and they pulled as hard as they could.

All of a sudden the hook came free from the rough stones. Up flew the rope and, with a **bump, bump, bump,** the three sillies fell flat on their backs!

As they lay there on the ground, dazed and confused, they looked up at the night sky and what did they see?

They saw the moon, of course.

"We did it," they cried. "We pulled the moon out of the well and it is back in the sky where it belongs!"

Pleased with their hard work, the silly family went back to their beds where they dreamed happy but hopelessly silly dreams!

The Twelve Dancing Princesses

There was once a king who had twelve beautiful daughters. They slept in one room and every night their father would lock their door. But every morning there were twelve pairs of worn-out shoes under their beds.

It was as if the princesses had been out all night dancing. But how could that be? It was a mystery no one could solve except the princesses, and they simply smiled whenever they were asked.

"Any man who discovers the secret of where the princesses go at night," proclaimed the king, "shall be granted one of my daughters in marriage. But," he warned, "anyone who fails after three nights will be punished by death."

Many suitors tried, but all failed to uncover the secret of the twelve princesses.

Now it happened that a soldier was passing through the kingdom when he met an old woman. Hearing that he would like to be the one to solve the mystery, the woman gave him some advice.

"When one of the princesses offers you some wine," she said, "pretend to drink it and then act as if you are sleeping deeply." And handing him a special cloak, she explained, "Wear this and you will become invisible so you can follow the princesses."

Later that night just before the king locked the door of the princesses' bedroom, the eldest princess gave the soldier a goblet of wine. Carefully pouring it away, he soon pretended to snore loudly.

"We have tricked another one!" laughed the princess as they all changed into their ballgowns and tied their new dancing shoes.

The eldest princess clapped her hands, and a trap door magically opened up beneath her feet. One by one the twelve princesses disappeared down the steps.

The soldier immediately sprang up and grabbed the cloak. Just as the old woman had predicted, he became invisible. But in his haste, he stepped on the hem of the dress of the youngest princess.

"Someone has pulled my dress," she cried loudly.

"Don't be silly," replied her sisters, "it's just a nail."

At the bottom of the stairs, a door opened out to a spectacular avenue of trees, each one bearing silver leaves that shimmered under the starlit sky.

Following closely behind the laughing princesses, the invisible soldier broke off a silver branch, which snapped loudly.

"See, we are being followed," cried the youngest princess. But her sisters were too excited to worry.

Leaving the silver trees behind, the happy princesses now ran daintily through an avenue of pure gold trees. It was a magnificent sight in the moonlight. The soldier followed, snapping off a golden branch.

Finally they reached the glittering diamond trees and to the invisible soldier, this was the most breathtaking sight of all. As the soldier snapped off a branch from a diamond tree, the youngest princess screamed. But her sisters only laughed more loudly as they ran toward the lake.

Lined up on the water were twelve little boats and in each was a prince ready to row the princesses across to the castle.

The soldier jumped into the boat with the youngest princess as the sound of trumpets filled the air.

Inside the castle, music and laughter rang out as the princesses danced with their handsome princes in the ballroom. The youngest princess was the only one feeling uneasy all evening.

Every time she lifted a goblet of wine, it was snatched out of her hand by the mischievous soldier. She tried in vain to warn her sisters, but they were only interested in having fun. They danced and danced until finally the cock crowed. Then the twelve princes rowed them back across the lake.

The soldier managed to run ahead and was back in bed snoring when the princesses returned to their room.

"We're safe!" whispered the eldest sister, checking up on the sleeping soldier. Happy but tired, the twelve princesses took off their tattered dancing shoes and were soon fast asleep.

The soldier followed the princesses again the next night, and on the third night he took a golden goblet from the castle as proof of where the sisters had been.

When he was summoned to the king after the final night, he was able to show him a silver branch, a gold branch, and a diamond branch, as well as the castle goblet.

The princesses's secret had finally been discovered, and the king was very grateful.

"I mean to keep my promise," he said. "Which of the princesses will you choose for your wife?" he asked the soldier.

"I am not a young man," replied the soldier, "so I think I will choose the eldest."

Soon they were married, and in time the soldier became king of the whole country. He ruled wisely and never forgot the old woman in the woods and her words of advice.

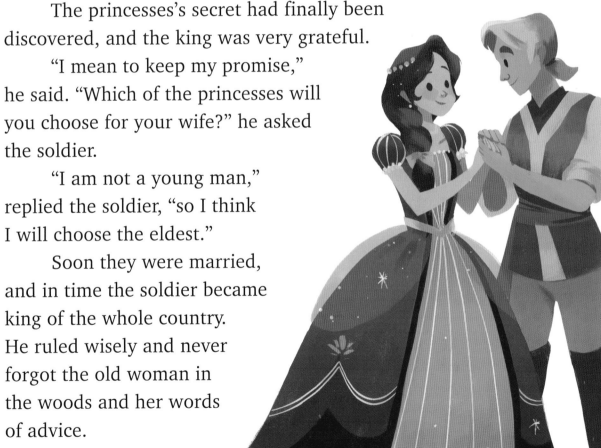

Rumpelstiltskin

Once upon a time, there was a poor miller who had just one daughter. He was very proud of her and he told many people about her virtues.

One day, the king rode through the village. The miller desperately wanted to impress the king. "Your Highness, my daughter is clever beyond compare," he said.

But the king took no notice.

"She can also spin straw into gold!" the miller lied.

"Your daughter must be very clever. Bring her to the palace tomorrow so I can see for myself," demanded the king.

The miller didn't dare disobey the king, so the next day he brought his daughter to the palace. The king led the girl to a room filled with straw. On the floor stood a stool and a spinning wheel.

"Spin this straw into gold by tomorrow morning, or you will be thrown into the dungeon," said the king. Then he left the room and locked the door.

The poor miller's daughter sat down on the stool and gazed at all the straw around her. She wept bitterly at the impossible task before her.

All of a sudden, the door sprang open and in came the strangest little man she had ever seen.

"Why are you crying?" he asked.

"I have to spin all this straw into gold before the morning, but I don't know how," replied the girl sadly.

"If you give me your pretty necklace, I will spin the straw into gold," said the strange little man.

"Oh, thank you!" gasped the girl, wiping away her tears and handing over her necklace.

The little man sat down in front of the spinning wheel and set to work.

All night long, the little man spun, and by morning the room was filled with reels of gold. And just as suddenly as he had appeared, the strange man disappeared.

When the king arrived, he was astonished to see so much gold.

"You have done very well," he said, "but I wonder if you can do the same thing again?"

He took the miller's daughter to a much bigger room. It, too, was filled with straw. More straw than she had ever seen!

"Spin this straw into gold by tomorrow morning, or you will be thrown into the dungeon," said the king, and once more he locked the girl in the room.

The miller's daughter was very frightened. The strange little man appeared before her again.

"Don't cry," he said. "Give me your shiny ring, and I will spin the straw into gold."

She handed over her ring gratefully, and the little man set to work immediately.

Once again, all the straw was turned into gold.

The king was thrilled. "If you can spin straw into gold again, you shall marry my son and become a queen!" cried the king.

The poor miller's daughter wept even more bitterly when the king left.

"Why are you crying?" said the little man, appearing for the third time. "You know that I will help you."

"But I have nothing left to give you," sobbed the girl.

"If you become queen," replied the little man, "I want you to promise to give me your first-born child."

The desperate miller's daughter agreed to the man's request. And once again, he spun all the straw into gold.

The king was so delighted when he saw all the gold the next day that he kept his promise. He introduced the Crown Prince to the miller's daughter, and they were soon married.

It wasn't long before the couple fell truly in love, and became king and queen of the land. The new queen was very happy and forgot all about the promise she had made to the strange little man who saved her from the dungeon.

A year later, the king and queen were blessed with a beautiful baby boy.

Then late one night, the little man appeared in the queen's bedroom as she watched over her sleeping baby.

"I'm here to collect your baby," he said. "Just as you promised."

The queen was horrified. "Oh, please, take all my jewels and money instead," she begged. "Not my son!"

"No," replied the little man. "You made a promise. But I will give you three days. If in that time you can guess my name, then you will keep your baby."

The desperate queen agreed. She sent messengers all over the kingdom to collect all the boys' names they could find.

That night, the strange man appeared again, and the queen read out the names she had gathered. But after each name he just laughed.

The next day, the queen sent her messengers out to find even more names, and that night she read out the new names when the little man appeared. But once again, the queen's guesses were wrong.

On the third day, the poor queen was in despair. It was getting late by the time her last messenger returned.

"Your Highness, I haven't found any new names," he said, "but as I was returning through the forest, I saw a little man leaping and dancing around a fire, singing a song. It went like this:

'The queen will never win my game,
 For Rumpelstiltskin is my name!'"

The queen was overjoyed!

When the little man appeared that night, the queen said, "Are you perhaps called … Rumpelstiltskin?"

The little man was furious. He stamped his foot so hard it went through the floor. Then, pulling on his leg until he was free, he stomped out of the room and was never heard from again.

The king and queen, and their son, lived happily ever after.

Snow White

One dark winter night, a young queen was sewing next to her bedroom window. When she looked up to gaze at the winter moon, her needle slipped and pricked her finger. A single drop of blood fell upon the snow on the windowsill.

She put down her sewing and watched the drop of blood spread out in the snow.

"How beautiful it looks against the white snow and the black of the windowsill," she said. "I wish I had a child with skin as white as snow, lips as red as blood, and hair of ebony black."

The queen's wish was granted! She gave birth to a little girl with milk-white skin, sweet red lips, and hair that shone as black as the night.

The king lifted the little princess into his arms. "I love her with all my heart," he said. "What shall we call her?"

"There is only one name that will do," said the queen. "She is our little Snow White."

The arrival of the royal baby should have been a time of great happiness, but sadly the queen suddenly fell ill and died, leaving the king to bring up his daughter alone.

After a year had passed, the king's advisors visited him.

"Your Majesty, it is time for you to marry again," said the chief advisor. "Princess Snow White needs a mother."

"Very well," he said in a quiet voice. "Find me a suitable bride and I will marry her."

A short time later, the kingdom celebrated the royal wedding. Everyone could see that the new queen was a beauty. But from the moment that she put on the royal crown, the new queen was unkind to everyone who served her.

"That queen spends all her time gazing into her golden mirror," said one of the ladies-in-waiting. "Surely she's tired of her reflection?"

The queen's mirror was enchanted. Every day the queen looked into it and asked a question:

"Mirror, mirror, on the wall,
Who is the fairest of them all?"

The mirror rippled. Then a voice spoke through the glass:

"The truth, my queen, I cannot hide,
You are the fairest, far and wide."

As the years passed, the queen grew more beautiful, and even more proud. But someone else in the kingdom was also growing more beautiful every day.

Snow White's ebony black hair fell down to her waist. She had porcelain skin and lips as red as berries.

One moonless night, the queen gazed into her enchanted mirror and asked, just as she had done a thousand times before:

"Mirror, mirror, on the wall,

Who is the fairest of them all?"

This time, however, there was a different reply:

"Indeed your beauty shines out bright,

But not as fair as young Snow White."

Every time she thought of Snow White her jealousy grew, until she felt there was only one solution. She sent for the royal huntsman.

"Take Snow White into the forest and kill her," she ordered. "Bring me the girl's heart. I want to know that she is gone forever."

The huntsman's heart ached, but he was scared of the queen.

The next day, he took Snow White deep into the forest. As they walked, the girl chattered and sang. She chased after butterflies and skipped ahead to pick flowers.

At last the huntsman stopped and took out his knife. "Now it is time," he whispered to himself. "I must kill this child."

When Snow White saw the knife she began to cry. "Leave me here," she begged. "I will never come back to the palace. Please."

The hunstsman couldn't bring himself to kill her. He let her go, and killed a deer instead. Now he had a heart to give the queen.

After a long time stumbling through the forest, Snow White pushed her way through a thicket and stepped out onto a path. There stood a house so small that if she stood on her tiptoes she could reach the upstairs windows.

"What a quaint little home!" said Snow White. She knocked on the door, but there was no answer. She pushed against it and it swung open.

"Maybe I can sleep here for a little while," she said.

She kicked off her shoes and crept quietly upstairs. There she saw seven beds lined up in a row! Snow White sank onto the nearest bed. Within seconds, she was asleep.

It was late when the cottage door swung open again, and seven dwarfs trooped inside. "Whose shoes are these?" asked one dwarf, gazing down at Snow White's slippers.

The dwarfs lit their candles and marched upstairs, furious. But as soon as their candlelight fell on Snow White, their anger melted.

"What a beautiful child," they all said.

"Don't wake her," said one of the dwarfs. "She looks tired. We can wait until the morning to ask who she is."

When Snow White tiptoed down the stairs the next morning, she found the seven dwarfs waiting for her.

"We saved you some of our breakfast," said one dwarf.

Snow White told the dwarfs about the queen's wicked plan.

"Stay with us," said the dwarfs. "We will keep you safe."

"Thank you!" Snow White smiled. "I would love to."

After a week, the dwarfs felt as if she had always lived there.

Then one night the queen decided to gaze in her mirror and asked her usual question. The reply was not what she was expecting:

"Through the forest, in mountain air,
Live seven dwarfs and a king's lost heir.
You may turn heads, but Snow White so true,
Is a thousand times more fair than you."

"Snow White is alive!" cried the queen. "I will never rest until I am once more the fairest in the land."

The next day, the queen disguised herself as an apple seller. The apples in her basket were red and shiny, but they were poisoned.

The queen made her way to the little cottage. She peeked in through a window and saw Snow White inside.

"Would you like to buy an apple or two, miss?" she asked.

"They do look tasty," thought Snow White. "Yes, please."

The queen handed her the poisoned apple and watched as the girl took a tiny bite. Snow White instantly dropped to the ground.

When the dwarfs got back to the cottage that evening, they found Snow White lying on the ground with the apple still gleaming in her hand.

"The wicked queen tricked her," they cried.

The dwarfs laid Snow White in a clear glass coffin at the top of the mountain, where the most beautiful flowers grew.

The next day, a young prince came riding along the track. When he saw Snow White lying in her glass case, he stopped.

"This might sound strange," he said, "but I have fallen in love. Please, let me take her back to my kingdom so that I can see her every day."

"If you truly love her, then you should take her to be with you," said the dwarfs.

As they lifted the coffin, the piece of apple that had caught in Snow White's throat was knocked loose. She took a deep breath and opened her eyes. The prince was the first thing she saw and she loved him at once.

"Oh, I am alive!" she cried.

The prince helped Snow White out of the glass coffin. Then he kneeled down before her.

"You do not know me yet," he said. "But I am already in love with you. Will you come back to my kingdom and become my wife?"

Snow White smiled, but before she could reply, the dwarfs raced up to her. Laughing and crying for joy, Snow White hugged each one of them tightly. Then she turned and took the prince's hand.

"Yes! I will marry you," she said. Snow White and the prince lived happily ever after.

When the queen heard, she smashed her magic mirror and was never seen again.

The Gingerbread Man

Once upon a time, a little old woman and a little old man lived by themselves in a little old cottage. One day the little old woman decided to bake a treat for the little old man.

"I'll make a special gingerbread man," she thought. She mixed all the ingredients together, rolled out the dough, cut out the gingerbread man, and popped him in the oven to bake.

After a while, the little old woman heard a strange voice.

"Let me out! I've finished baking and it's hot in here!"

The little old woman looked around. She was confused. "I must be hearing voices!" she chuckled to herself.

She opened the oven door and nearly fell over in surprise when the little gingerbread man jumped off the baking tray, rushed past her, and ran out through the front door.

"Come back," cried the little old woman. "We want to eat you!"

But the gingerbread man was too fast for the little old woman. He ran into the garden and past the little old man.

"Stop!" cried the little old man, setting down his wheelbarrow. "I want to eat you!"

But the little gingerbread man was already halfway down the road outside the little old cottage. He was very fast, and the little old woman and the little old man were very slow.

"Stop! Stop!" they wheezed, out of breath, as they ran down the road.

The gingerbread man darted under a fence into a field, singing as he went:

"Run, run, as fast as you can.
You can't catch me, I'm the gingerbread man!"

As the gingerbread man ran through the field, he passed a pig.

"Stop!" snorted the pig. "I want to eat you!"

"I've run away from a little old woman and a little old man, and I can run away from you," said the gingerbread man.

And he ran even faster, followed by the little old woman, the little old man, and the pig.

Soon the little gingerbread man met a cow.

"You smell scrumptious!" mooed the cow. "Stop, little man, I want to eat you!"

But the gingerbread man just ran faster. "I've run away from a little old woman, a little old man, and a pig, and I can run away from you," he cried.

The cow started to run after the gingerbread man, but he sprinted past her through the tall grass in the field, singing out:

"Run, run, as fast as you can.

You can't catch me, I'm the gingerbread man!"

The little old woman, the little old man, the pig, and the cow ran and ran, but none of them could catch the gingerbread man.

In the next field, the gingerbread man met a horse.

"You look yummy!" neighed the horse. "Stop, little man, I want to eat you!"

But the gingerbread man just ran faster. "I have run away from a little old woman, a little old man, a pig, and a cow, and I can run away from you!" he cried.

The horse started to gallop after the gingerbread man, but he was already halfway across the field. He turned and waved at the horse as he sang out:

"Run, run, as fast as you can.
You can't catch me, I'm the gingerbread man!"

The little old woman, the little old man, the pig, the cow, and the horse ran and ran, but none of them could catch the little gingerbread man.

The little gingerbread man squeezed through a hedge and ran on, faster and faster, along a path through a shady wood. He grinned, feeling very pleased with himself.

"No one can catch me!" he giggled.

But just a little further on down the woodland path, the gingerbread man came to an abrupt stop. There before him flowed a wide river, completely blocking his way.

While the little gingerbread man was wondering how he was going to get across the river, a sly old fox came up to him.

"Hello, little man," said the fox, licking his lips. "You look like you could use some help."

"Oh yes, please," cried the gingerbread man. "I've run away from a little old woman, a little old man, a pig, a cow, and a horse, and I need to get across this river so that I can keep on running. And I can't swim!"

"Well, jump on my back, and I'll carry you across the river," grinned the sly old fox. "You'll be safe and dry."

So the little gingerbread man climbed onto the fox's tail and the fox began to swim across the river.

After a while, the fox said, "You're too heavy for my tail. Jump onto my back."

The little gingerbread man ran lightly down the fox's tail and jumped onto his back, clinging tightly onto his fur.

Soon, the fox said, "You're too heavy for my back. Jump onto my nose."

The little gingerbread man did as he was told and jumped onto the fox's nose.

At last, they reached the other side of the river. The little gingerbread man was just about to jump to the ground when the hungry fox threw back his head.

The gingerbread man suddenly found himself tossed high in the air. Then down he fell and **Snap!** went the mouth of the sly old fox.

And that was the end of the little gingerbread man!

Songs and Rhymes

The Owl and the Pussycat

The Owl and the Pussycat went to sea
In a beautiful pea-green boat,
They took some honey, and plenty of money,
Wrapped up in a five pound note.
The Owl looked up to the stars above,
And sang to a small guitar,
"Oh lovely, Pussy! Oh Pussy, my love,
What a beautiful Pussy you are, you are, you are,
What a beautiful Pussy you are."

Pussy said to the Owl, "You elegant fowl,
How charmingly sweet you sing.
Oh let us be married, too long we have tarried;
But what shall we do for a ring?"
They sailed away, for a year and a day,
To the land where the Bong tree grows,
And there in a wood a Piggy-wig stood
With a ring at the end of his nose, his nose, his nose,
With a ring at the end of his nose.

"Dear Pig, are you willing to sell for one shilling your ring?"
Said the Piggy, "I will."
So they took it away, and were married next day
By the Turkey who lives on the hill.
They dined on mince, and slices of quince,
Which they ate with a runcible spoon.
And hand in hand, on the edge of the sand,
They danced by the light of the moon, the moon, the moon,
They danced by the light of the moon.

All Through the Night

Sleep, my child, and peace attend thee,
All through the night.
Guardian angels God will send thee,
All through the night.
Soft the drowsy hours are creeping,
Hill and dale in slumber sleeping
I my loved ones' watch am keeping,
All through the night.

Angels watching, e'er around thee,
All through the night.
Midnight slumber close surround thee,
All through the night.
Soft the drowsy hours are creeping,
Hill and dale in slumber sleeping
I my loved ones' watch am keeping,
All through the night.

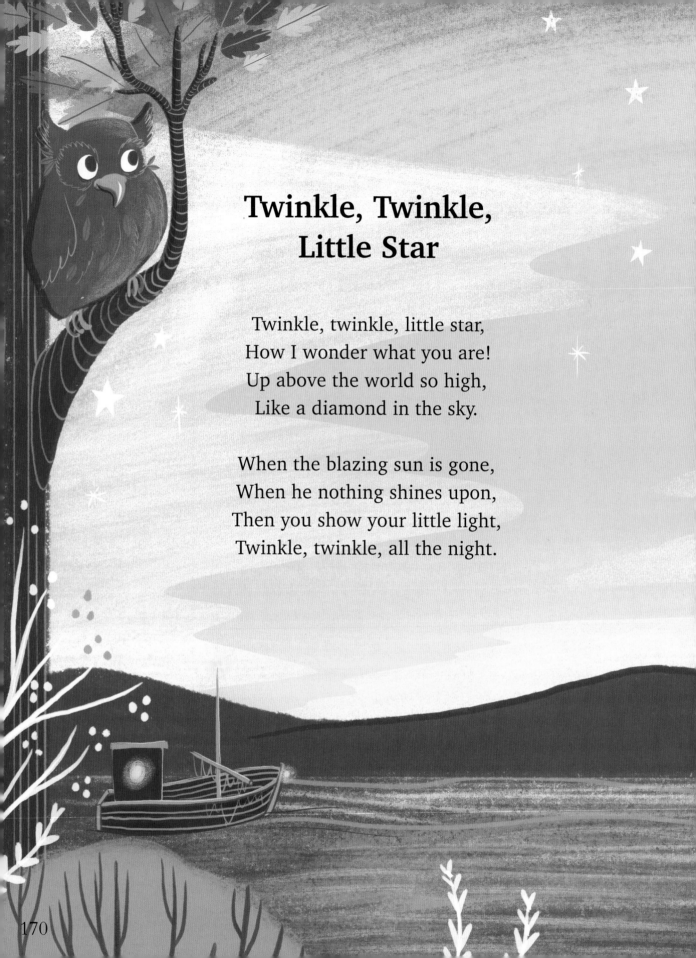

Twinkle, Twinkle, Little Star

Twinkle, twinkle, little star,
How I wonder what you are!
Up above the world so high,
Like a diamond in the sky.

When the blazing sun is gone,
When he nothing shines upon,
Then you show your little light,
Twinkle, twinkle, all the night.

Then the traveler in the dark,
Thanks you for your tiny spark.
He could not see which way to go,
If you did not twinkle so.

In the dark blue sky you keep,
And often through my curtains peep,
For you never shut your eye,
Till the sun is in the sky.

As your bright and tiny spark,
Lights the traveller in the dark—
Though I know not what you are,
Twinkle, twinkle, little star.

Now the Day Is Over

Now the day is over,
Night is drawing nigh;
Shadows of the evening
Steal across the sky.

Now the darkness gathers,
Stars begin to peep,
Birds and beasts and flowers
Soon will be asleep.

Jesus, give the weary
Calm and sweet repose;
With your tenderest blessing
May my eyelids close.

Grant to little children
Visions bright of Thee;
Guard the sailors tossing
On the deep-blue sea.

Oranges and Lemons

"Oranges and lemons,"
Say the bells of St. Clements.

"You owe me five farthings,"
Say the bells of St. Martins.

"When will you pay me?"
Say the bells of Old Bailey.

"When I grow rich,"
Say the bells of Shoreditch.

"When will that be?"
Say the bells of Stepney.

"I do not know,"
Says the great bell at Bow.

Wynken, Blynken, and Nod

Wynken, Blynken, and Nod one night
Sailed off in a wooden shoe,
Sailed on a river of crystal light
Into a sea of dew.
"Where are you going, and what do you wish?"
The old moon asked the three.
"We have come to fish for the herring fish
That live in this beautiful sea;
Nets of silver and gold have we,"
Said Wynken,
Blynken,
And Nod.

The old moon laughed and sang a song,
As they rocked in the wooden shoe;
And the wind that sped them all night long
Ruffled the waves of dew;
The little stars were the herring fish
That lived in the beautiful sea.
"Now cast your nets wherever you wish,
Never afraid are we!"
So cried the stars to the fishermen three:
Wynken,
Blynken,
And Nod.

All night long their nets they threw
To the stars in the twinkling foam,
Then down from the skies came the wooden shoe,
Bringing the fishermen home.
'Twas all so pretty a sail, it seemed
As if it could not be.
And some folk thought 'twas a dream they'd dreamed
Of sailing that beautiful sea.
But I shall name you the fishermen three:
Wynken,
Blynken,
And Nod.

Wynken and Blynken are two little eyes,
And Nod is a little head,
And the wooden shoe that sailed the skies
Is a wee one's trundle bed.
So shut your eyes while Mother sings
Of wonderful sights that be,
And you shall see the beautiful things
As you rock in the misty sea
Where the old shoe rocked the fishermen three:
Wynken,
Blynken,
And Nod.

Wee Willie Winkie

Wee Willie Winkie
Runs through the town,
Upstairs and downstairs
In his nightgown.
Rapping at the window,
Crying through the lock,
"Are the children all in bed?
It's past eight o'clock."

Rock-a-Bye, Baby

Rock-a-bye, baby, on the treetop,
When the wind blows, the cradle will rock;
When the bough breaks, the cradle will fall;
Down will come baby, cradle and all.

Star Light, Star Bright

Star light, star bright,
First star I see tonight,
I wish I may, I wish I might,
Have this wish I wish tonight.

Golden Slumbers

Golden slumbers kiss your eyes,
Smiles await you when you rise.
Sleep, pretty baby, do not cry,
And I will sing a lullaby.

Cares you know not, therefore sleep,
While over you a watch I'll keep.
Sleep, pretty darling, do not cry,
And I will sing a lullaby.

Aiken Drum

There was a man lived in the moon,
Lived in the moon, lived in the moon,
There was a man lived in the moon,
And his name was Aiken Drum.

And he played upon a ladle,
A ladle, a ladle,
And he played upon a ladle,
And his name was Aiken Drum.

And his hat was made of good cream cheese,
Good cream cheese, good cream cheese,
And his hat was made of good cream cheese,
And his name was Aiken Drum.

And his coat was made of good roast beef,
Good roast beef, good roast beef,
And his coat was made of good roast beef,
And his name was Aiken Drum.

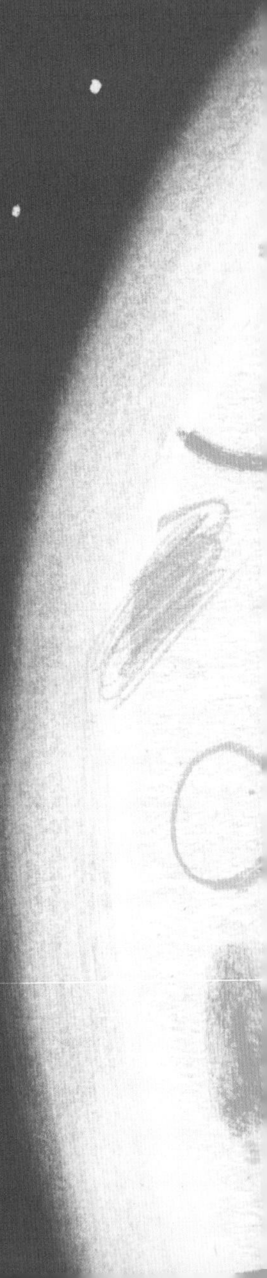

And his buttons were made of penny loaves,
Penny loaves, penny loaves,
And his buttons made of penny loaves,
And his name was Aiken Drum.

And his waistcoat was made of crust pies,
Crust pies, crust pies,
And his waistcoat was made of crust pies,
And his name was Aiken Drum.

And his breeches made of haggis bags,
Haggis bags, haggis bags,
And his breeches made of haggis bags,
And his name was Aiken Drum.

The Grand Old Duke of York

The grand old Duke of York,
He had ten thousand men,
He marched them up to the top of the hill,
And he marched them down again.

When they were up, they were up,
And when they were down, they were down,
And when they were only halfway up,
They were neither up nor down.

Rub-a-Dub-Dub

Rub-a-dub-dub,
Three men in a tub,
And how do you think they got there?
The butcher, the baker,
The candlestick maker,
They all jumped out of a rotten potato,
It was enough to make a man stare.

How Many Miles to Babylon?

How many miles to Babylon?
Three score and ten.
Can I get there by candlelight?
Yes, and back again.
If your heels are nimble and light,
You may get there by candlelight.

Brahms's Lullaby

Lullaby and good night,
In the skies, stars bright
With lilies over spread
Is baby's wee bed.
Lay thee down now and rest,
May thy slumber be blessed.

Lullaby and good night,
Thy mother's delight,
Bright angels beside
My darling abide.
They will guard thee at rest,
Thou shalt wake on my breast.

The
end